GHOSTS REVISITED 4

William P. Robertson

The tales in this book come from local folklore, friends' testimonies, and internet research. They are as factual as the author could make them although other versions are sometimes told.

Published by **BookBaby**
www.bookbaby.com

CONTENTS

CREDITS

Beginning the Casey's story is a postcard pic of the original Limestone House. The second Casey's Restaurant photo was provided by Tim Reed.

The surveillance photo of the parlor room ghost is courtesy of the Jefferson County History Center. The crow and buzzard pics were taken by the "Birdman," Bob Burns. The Gibsonia, PA haunted house photo was submitted by Rene Yates.

Karl Schellhammer contributed the letter from famed ghost hunter, Hans Holzer, and the 451 Pierson Run Road house pic. Brian Edgcomb supplied the King House photos. Julie Boozer sent a photograph of the first Scandia church along its history. Lastly, Bob Whiteman donated the Tally Ho ghost pic. All other photos are by William P. Robertson.

A special thanks goes out to Marcie Schellhammer, Assistant Managing Editor of the *Bradford Era*, for furnishing leads for several ghost stories that appear in this collection.

The portrait of Thomas Litch hangs in the parlor room at the Jefferson County History Center in Brookville, PA.

A note of appreciation is due to curator, Gail Thompson, and city historian, Jim Griffith, of the Salamanca Historical Society for digging up background info used in the Dudley Hotel piece.

A tip of the cap is sent to Cindy Pascarella, too, for providing the creepy carriage that appears on the cover. It made the perfect prop! Cindy is manager of the Main Street Mercantile in Bradford, PA where the carriage is still for sale.

Thanks also to artist, David Cox, for creating the eerie cover. David may be contacted at dlcox1972@gmail.com.

CASEY'S RESTAURANT

Built by Henry Renner in 1865, Casey's Restaurant was originally known as the Limestone House and sat across the railroad tracks from the town of Limestone, New York. In its early days, it contained fourteen hotel rooms to accommodate visitors who arrived by train. One of those visitors was President Woodrow Wilson!

In 1950, retired golf pro, Pat Burke, and his wife, Dorothy, purchased the business from Jim Casey and moved into the second floor to raise their family. Below, they opened a saloon and eating place that catered to rowdy oilfield workers. Sawdust was scattered across the floor to protect it from muddy boots and cigarette butts tossed there at random. When trains would chug past, every bottle on the bar would rattle, causing an awful ruckus.

It wasn't until the Burkes began serving tasty sirloin steaks at their restaurant that they attracted a more sophisticated clientele. They made it a practice to present the steak to the patron before cooking it to his or her specifications. Soon, their establishment was filled to capacity with hungry families and weekend crowds.

The owners also hired Phil English to play piano and keep the customers entertained. He hosted a party every night and became equally famous for his evening performances and his Shades of Night drink that contained vodka, gin, and crème de menthe, topped with a cherry. Phil's fame spread even farther when a photo of him leading a spirited sing-along was featured in the December 1959 issue of *Life* magazine.

At the height of the restaurant's success, Pat and Dorothy were forced to move their business to Bailey Drive across from Western Steer Market due to the construction of U.S. Route 219 through Limestone. Before occupying it, they refurbished a building formerly owned by Art Zirkle that dated back to the 1850s. They also attached the façade and curved awning from the original Casey's onto the front to attract customers to their new venue. Dorothy died of a heart attack some years later while performing her usual duties.

The establishment continued to thrive through the 1980s. According to Kirk Schellhammer, who worked as busboy in the latter years of that decade, Casey's was then divided into three distinct areas. The ground floor housed the dining room, the rathskeller in the basement served as the piano bar, while the second floor was used for storage and contained a dressing room for employees. Kirk hadn't worked there long, however, before he also learned that the restaurant was haunted!

Schellhammer found the basement especially disturbing. On several occasions while cleaning up after the pianist went home, he heard "someone" whisper his name. He often heard the door to the ground floor open above him, too. The floor would then creak as footsteps crossed to the office. Then that door also grated open. Going upstairs to investigate, he'd find no one else in the building.

Another strange occurrence happened to Kirk when he carted unneeded chairs up to the second floor. Returning from storage, he glanced into the dressing room to see a misty apparition. She was seated at a table and dressed in a full-length teal gown. When she began to turn her head toward him, Kirk sprinted down the stairs, maybe touching two of them, before bursting out of breath into the dining room.

"So you've seen Dorothy, have you?" asked a bemused older waitress.

"Yes, I did!" gasped Schellhammer. "How did you know?"

"Just a sneaking suspicion," croaked the woman, crossing herself like the good Catholic she was.

MEMORIAL SPRING

Gilbert Mohney, Howard F. May, Basil Bogush, Ross Hollobaugh, Andrew Stephanic, Stephen Jacofsky, John F. Boring, and George W. Vogel worked for the Civilian Conservation Corps and were stationed at Camp S-132 near Emporium, Pennsylvania. The CCC provided work for unemployed unmarried men between the ages of seventeen and twenty-eight during the Great Depression of the 1930s. Their typical jobs consisted of road building, stream improvement, and erosion control.

On October 19, 1938, though, the boys were engaged in a much more dangerous endeavor when a wildfire swept through the woods of Jerry Run and Lick Island. With flames crackling around them, they battled the blaze with shoveled dirt and fire lanes slashed in the brush. They toiled for hours, and had the fire nearly contained, when the unfortunate eight got caught in a backdraft. Boxed in by a wall of fire, they were roasted alive as they screamed, and their flesh sizzled!

The sacrifice of these brave boys lives on, though, at the Memorial Spring located along Route 120 south of Emporium. The spring is well manicured, and a plaque in their honor is fitted into solid stone. On dark nights, their spirits continue to shine, too. Eight lights float across the mountain top above, plainly seen by all who care to notice them.

130 JACKSON AVENUE

130 Jackson Avenue in Bradford, Pennsylvania served for a number of years as a boys' group home. One of the female employees was always on edge while working there at night and refused to stay past eleven p.m. when her shift was over. She often got an eerie feeling, as well, when loud cars would screech their brakes on the street outside. Could the place be haunted by someone killed in a car crash? Perhaps that's the reason this mansion was sold to a private individual for way under market value. . .

JACQUINS POND

Jacquins Pond is a wildlife management area used by hunters, hikers, and fishermen. In 1977, the Department of Environmental Conservation purchased this property located on Caflisch Road near Clymer, New York. The thirty acres are designated as wetlands habitat, but they also house a spooky, haunted morass frequented by those drawn to the supernatural.

According to legend, a bus driver named George sped to Jacquins Pond after his vehicle struck and killed a young boy who darted out in front of him. He was so remorseful he rode for hours along the narrow dirt roads that cut through the area. After rumbling over the third bridge he encountered in a creepy swamp, he parked and shot himself through the head.

If one stops at the third bridge today, he will see George's ghost after repeating the dead man's name three times. George will then lock the visitor's car doors before fading with a wicked laugh into the nearby woods. Farther down, this road splits into two paths. One is of light and the other of darkness. The dark path is where teens go to contemplate their own suicides.

SCANDIA CHURCH

Swedish immigrants swarmed into Scandia, Pennsylvania in the 1870s seeking freedom from the land barons that enslaved them in their home country. They established farms and a place of worship they called Scandia Swedish Mission Church.

The original sanctuary had a curved roof that landing demons would slide down to crash in the yard outside, preventing evil from entering the building. The roof was also topped by a weathervane hammered from a sawblade in the blacksmith shop across the road. This designated the church as a Protestant one. The Catholics displayed crosses on their buildings.

Due to the growing population, a bigger sanctuary was built in 1892. It was started after crops had been harvested in October and was finished by Christmas. A year later, a cyclone swooped down and knocked the church off its foundation. The hardy Swedes reset it using a team of horses.

It was during this time that each member of the church family was assigned a plot in the graveyard that stretched across the side lawn up to the walls of the sanctuary. The farmers had little money for tombstones, so most of the graves were unmarked. Dead infants were interred without coffins, as well, due to financial concerns.

A new addition and a parking lot were added in the 1980s to what was then known as the Scandia Evangelical Covenant Church. That's when weird things began to happen. Parishioners, for example, would hear loud voices coming from an adjoining room. They'd rush to join in on the conversation only to find no one there.

A former pastor got a scare, too. He left his bible in the sanctuary while retreating to his office for some sermon notes. When he returned moments later, the book had disappeared from the pulpit. After a thorough search, he found it perched on a window ledge and shivered at the discovery. He was alone in the building at the time.

The ladies of the church also refused to go there at night by themselves. That was after they heard the locked basement door creak open while those who attended their meeting were still upstairs. They came to a whispered conclusion that their ancestors' spirits weren't happy. Their unmarked graves had been built and paved over during the '80s remodeling.

Site of Old
Scandia Cemetery (1877)

...which stretched east from the Church sanctuary to the Grange Hall. Among the Swedish immigrants buried here is Anders Olsson (1821 – 1904). When this cemetery filled, The New Cemetery was opened (1900).

LITCH HOUSE

The Litch House legend reads like the plot of an H. P. Lovecraft story. Ken and Jeannie Petardi recently bought the old mansion and are now refurbishing it. It sits on a bluff at 16 Taylor Street in Brookville, Pennsylvania and was built in the Stick Style of architecture. The three-story tower with arched windows and a convex roof is beautiful to behold. Cross-shaped ornaments under the eaves and the three-bay porch are impressive, as well. The trees that hem the place in, though, hint at the evil that permeates it.

The house was originally constructed by Thomas Litch in the 1850s to overlook the steam-powered sawmills he owned on North Fork Creek. He came to Jefferson County from Pittsburgh where he accumulated a fortune building steam engines and riverboats. The lumber industry looked even more lucrative to the entrepreneur, and he tugged at his beard gleefully, thinking of all the money he would make.

To supply his mills with timber, Litch ignored advice from the locals and bought up a large tract of pine woods that Indians swore was inhabited by demons. Some say he mingled with those spirits and embraced their evil power. Others whisper that Litch made a pact with Satan himself. The spot where the devil trod near the family's backyard guesthouse has since remained barren. No snow will stay on it no matter how frigid the temperature.

Thomas' youngest son, Edward, also spent much time wandering about the woods that surrounded the Litch property. When his father threatened to send him back to Pittsburgh, he ran off and lived with the Iroquois for over a month.

Upon returning to Brookville, he ambled around the village raving about spirits that inhabited rocks and trees. Edward then locked himself up in the guesthouse and refused to return to his father's mansion.

Master Litch is still said to haunt the upper rooms of his stately home where he walks through walls at his pleasure. The walls were built of lumber harvested from the evil trees. Their essence festers. Forever. . .

JEFFERSON COUNTY HISTORY CENTER

Ken Burkett is the Executive Director of the Jefferson County History Center located at 172-176 Main Street in Brookville, Pennsylvania. Although he doesn't believe in ghosts, he has some strange tales to tell.

The first incident occurred at the Civil War display the History Center had erected to honor local GAR soldiers. Although the burglar alarm wasn't tripped in the building, Ken arrived at 6:30 one morning to find motion lights flashing and period music blaring. That only happened when someone entered the exhibit room. Burkett immediately searched the premises from top to bottom, but no one else was there!

The director discovered a second enigma at their Prohibition still display. An empty jug of Blackbird Distillery whiskey (locked in a showcase) was one of the props used. Burkett found the jug upside down one day with the removed cap sitting above it on a shelf. Ken couldn't believe it, because HE had the only key to the display case!

The most puzzling occurrence, though, took place in the parlor room upstairs where a sensor cam and motion activated lights were installed to protect the valuable antiques. On November 11, 2017 at 2:18 a.m., the lights snapped on, and the camera began taking photos in quick succession. The third pic caught a wispy object, resembling the edge of an old-fashioned dress, floating above the piano. It was presumed by superstitious staff members that they had captured on film none other than Clara Mulholland London. In 1893, Clara died in this same room after giving birth to a daughter. Her portrait hangs to the left of the closed gallery door that the figure had somehow glided through!

CROSBY'S MINI MART

Eileen Klenk was a special person. She had red hair and a smile for everyone. As a Wiccan, she was deeply spiritual and believed in holistic medicine. She was beloved by her neighbors for all the kind things she did for them like saving dogfood coupons for a man who had a voracious black lab. When she left for work on March 22, 1991, a terrible fate awaited her.

Eileen was a clerk at the since-closed Crosby's Mini Mart on South Kendall Avenue in Bradford, Pennsylvania. She noticed a vehicle parked across the road from the store when she entered but didn't have time to give it a second thought. She had barely put on her apron before she was swamped by a bevy of regular customers. She chatted happily with them as they paid for gas or bought Pennsylvania lottery tickets. She loved her job and brought much warmth to the people she served.

When things finally quieted down, a furtive man slipped into the mini mart. With a shiver, Eileen stepped from behind the counter to track the stranger's movements. He whipped suddenly around, brandishing a knife he drew from his coat pocket. Without a word, he began plunging the blade into the neck, chest, and abdomen of the shocked clerk. Before she could even scream, he stabbed her multiple times until she crumpled lifeless to the floor. Then he ransacked the cash register, grabbed himself a Coke, and sneered down at his bloody victim as he exited the building.

The first officer to arrive at the murder scene was from the Foster Township Police Department. He was so affected by the brutality of the killing that he reportedly suffered a nervous breakdown once more help arrived. The sight of Eileen's rent corpse was more than he could handle. He turned in his resignation after a year of counseling to follow less disturbing pursuits.

Through a description of the fleeing killer from a witness pulling up to the gas pumps, he was later identified as Louis Roach. Blood evidence found on Roach the next morning sealed his guilt. He was sentenced to life in prison after an emotional trial and died twenty-nine years later in his jail cell. Ironically, the killer might never have been caught had he not stopped on his way home at the Golden Eagle Hotel in Eldred for a beer. He was full of arrogance and still dripping with gore, so a suspicious patron called 911 to report him.

An eerie pall hung over Crosby's Mini Mart after Eileen Klenk's murder. Many believed that they saw her flitting through the back aisles of the store combing her abundant red hair. Others felt a cold breeze rush past them accompanied by a distinct jingle. Eileen always wore at least thirty bracelets that rattled when she walked. Even in death, bangles were her trademark.

EAST OTTO CEMETERY

Founded in 1854, the farming community of East Otto, New York is located in Cattaraugus County on County Route 12. The town cemetery is built atop a steep hill cut with dips and gullies. It's flanked by a row of ancient, gnarled maples while tulip trees, blotched with lichen, are spooky to behold. Some tombstones dating back to the 1850s have tumbled down. One grim stone marks the burial place of a War of 1812 veteran. With shadows entombing the oldest section of the graveyard even on the brightest days, one wonders if the iron fence was erected along the road to keep vandals out or the interred in!

When darkness falls, a gristly drama unfolds in this burial ground night after night that the locals have witnessed for years. Following a cacophony of shrieks, two headless women totter from the mist, wispy and horrible to behold. A swishing sound that's just as eerie grows louder with each passing second. It's made by a grim male phantom viciously wielding an ax. He strides forward with purpose and is covered in his victims' blood. No one knows why these specters are here. No one stays long enough to try and identify the killer!

A GIBSONIA HAUNTING

Thomas Datt was born in 1885 and took up farming for a trade like his father, grandfather, and great grandfather before him. After marrying Myrtle Magee, he ordered a Sears catalog build-by-numbers house that he constructed with the help of his neighbors. It was an eight-room, two-story structure located at 6029 Valencia Road in Gibsonia, Pennsylvania. It had old-fashioned gas lamps and cozy fireplaces for heat.

Datt made a good living growing wheat and corn. Added income came from his prize herd of Holstein cattle and the threshing machine he and his brother used to harvest his neighbors' crops. While burning off a field one spring, he spilled accelerant on his pants, and flames began licking up his legs. Instead of rolling on the ground to extinguish the fire, he sprinted in a panic for a nearby creek. His running only quickened his death as he burned to a crisp far short of the gurgling stream. He was eighty-three on that fateful day—Wednesday, March 26, 1969.

Rene Yates and her husband bought the Datt house from Myrtle in 1973. On the night they moved into their new home, they heard heavy footsteps reverberating up the stairs to the first landing. Her husband leaped out of bed and flung open the door to see who was there. Although the footsteps stopped, they didn't go up or down, either. The intruder had simply vanished into thin air!

On the second night, Rene stopped by her young sons' room to check on them. She softly opened the door and peeked inside to find the place in a shambles. Although she hadn't heard the slightest commotion, the boys' beds and furniture were turned upside down and their clothes emptied from their dresser drawers. It looked like a hurricane had hit the place, and yet the kids were sound asleep lying on their mattresses on the floor. They were still covered with their blankets, too, and were oblivious to the wrecking of their room.

After Rene's husband left her a year later, she learned who was responsible for the chaos in her house. She was half asleep one night when she heard someone entering her bedroom. She knew it couldn't be her children, for they were warned to knock before coming in. Groggily, she raised her head from her pillow to see the solid, charred form of a shadow man. When she turned on the light, the wraith walked straight through the side of her armoire and disappeared. It was Tom Datt who had come calling. Rene slept with the lights on for a month afterward, because meeting him face-to-face was overwhelming.

Tom, though, never hurt her or her children. He basically enjoyed playing pranks like turning on water faucets or snapping the lights on and off. One time, he did scare Rene's oldest son who said a man grabbed him by the ankle during the night. He knew it was a man's hand because of its roughness. When he screamed, the hand let go of him.

On another occasion, Rene's daughter was peeling potatoes in the kitchen just before supper. It was a hot summer evening, and she had a fan blowing on her legs. Suddenly, the fan stopped, and the girl gasped in disbelief while watching the switch flip off. It wasn't a glitch in the electricity, because the clock kept ticking in the corner. Before she could yell to her mom, the switch turned on again as if it had a will of its own.

Neighbors got their share of scares, too, while visiting Rene's residence. One afternoon, a young mother came over for coffee. She had just settled in at the kitchen table when she heard the outside door creak open.

"Darn kids!" exclaimed the visitor. "Can't get away from them anywhere."

As the door slammed shut, Rene and her friend turned to find no one there. A moment later, the cellar door opened and closed. Again, no one visible worked the handle.

"You know, I do kind of miss my children," croaked the alarmed mother. "See you later, Rene."

Another time, local teenagers decided to have a séance in the house. One girl removed the cross from around her neck and set it on the living room coffee table. Then the kids trooped upstairs to the hall and sat in a circle around a lit candle. Hearing a big bang below them, they rose white-faced and flew down the stairs. An upholstered chair had levitated across the living room to crash upside down in a far corner. When they saw their friend's crucifix lying on the rug beneath it, all thoughts of séances were immediately forgotten!

The last time Rene saw Tom Datt's ghost was on a Halloween night. His charred, solid form walked straight through the door into her bedroom. She had lived in the house for twenty-three years and now considered him a friend. When he sensed she was no longer afraid of him, he backed out the way he had come without attempting one scare tactic. That was in 1996. Rene moved to New York State soon after with her new husband, Rob.

451 PIERSON RUN ROAD

Karl Schellhammer spent his early youth living at 451 Pierson Run Road located in the suburbs of Pittsburgh, Pennsylvania. Half of the house had caught on fire, and the inside was gutted when Karl's father bought it. During the renovation, a chimney was demolished, and a pair of baby shoes was found inside. The sight of them gave all six children the chills.

Mrs. Schellhammer was attuned to the supernatural and frequently saw shadow figures wandering the hallways of their home. Her son, Michael, had an eerie encounter with one of them while fumbling to find the light switch in his dark bedroom. Suddenly, a glowing hand appeared on the wall that guided him directly to the switch. Then their grandma got a fright shortly after. She was pinned to her bed by an unseen entity that wouldn't let her up!

Karl had an equally eerie experience while engaging in a nighttime pillow fight with his cousin. With the shimmer of streetlights coming through the window to guide him, Schellhammer swung at the dodging outline of his adversary. When his pillow went straight through the figure, he let out a shriek and scrambled into the hall. There he saw his cousin returning from the bathroom. What he'd been battling couldn't be defined as "human."

Karl's sister, Jerrianne, had the worst of it living on Pierson Run Road. She sensed things and was tormented by them. It got so bad that Mrs. Schellhammer sent a letter to famed parapsychologist, Hans Holzer, to consult with him about her five-year-old daughter. Holzer replied forthwith and warned Mrs. S. to watch Jerrianne carefully and to keep him apprised of the situation. His letter can be seen on the next page.

HANS HOLZER, PARAPSYCHOLOGIST
Director
140 RIVERSIDE DRIVE · NEW YORK, N. Y. 10024

EST. 1962

Dear Correspondent,

Thank you for getting in touch with me.

If you wish to report a psychic experience,ESP,a haunting,
or other unusual happening,please write me about it - type
if you can - giving concise facts about the events,including
all the names,professions,ages and other data of anyone mentioned by you in your accounts,including yourself,and your own
background.

If your case involves a haunted house,facts about previous
owners of the place and the question whether a violent or
tragic death may have occurred there at any time is also of
interest.

All reports sent to me will be used as part of my files; in the
event that you do not wish to have your full name used,write
me to that effect; your address remains confidential in any
event.

If your case is urgent or requires my personal visit I will
undertake it,at no cost to you,of course,whenever I am in
your area and time allows.

If you are wondering where you may obtain my books: your local
bookstore,or directly from Hawthorn Books(70 Fifth Avenue
New York,N.Y.) - ESP AND YOU;PREDICTIONS:FACT OR FALLACY? -
and from Bobbs-Merrill (4300 West 62 Street,Indianapolis,Ind.)
-GHOST HUNTER,GHOSTS I'VE MET,YANKEE GHOSTS,THE LIVELY GHOSTS
OF IRELAND,GHOSTS OF THE GOLDEN WEST - some of which are
also available in paperback. If you're inquiring about mediums
or seances,I can't help you,but some mediums are mentioned in
my books.I cannot discuss any questions other than those
relating to an actual case of your own you wish to report
to me. General discussions or questions are answered in my
books.

Sincerely,

HANS HOLZER

If you like,if it comes up
with names, place, dates - let
me know. - Keep an eye on this.
What is her name?
H.H.

1167 EAST MAIN STREET

Karl Schellhammer has lived at the above address since 1977, and his family has had numerous spooky encounters inside this house. His mother was the first to be frightened by a shadow man that lurks in the basement. Their neighbor thinks he was probably the victim of a hit-and-run that occurred out front on East Main Street in the 1940s. The man was walking along the road when struck by a car that sped off leaving him to die in the front yard. His body wasn't found until the next morning, long after his soul found refuge in the damp confines of the cellar.

Another ghost has been seen by visiting grandchildren. After playing outside all morning, they always went upstairs to take a nap. Emily Schellhammer saw this spirit when she woke to see it rocking in the chair beside her bed. It was an elderly woman dressed in old-fashioned clothes with an afghan on its lap. It smiled gently down at Emily and seemed to be knitting as it quietly swayed so as not to disturb the child.

Later, Emily's grandmother told her not to be afraid of the ghost. "It won't hurt you," assured Grandma. "It watches you kids to make sure you're safe."

The third specter to haunt 1167 East Main Street is Karl's deceased father. The family dogs will often stare at "nothing" and wag their tails to acknowledge Mr. S.'s presence.

Karl remembers how much his dad loved to reload shells, a passion he shares. In the wee hours of the morning, Karl often goes into the reloading room to work. On one occasion, he kept messing up, because he could barely keep his eyes open. Over and over he tried to pour gunpowder into the brass shell casings he had lined up in a cartridge holder. The powder seemed to go everywhere but where it was supposed to.

Suddenly, the shells flipped off the reloading bench to scatter across the floor. In shocked surprise, Karl stood up and yelped, "Alright, Dad, I'm going to bed! You won't need to remind me twice."

544 DERRICK ROAD

With the help of a midwife, a young mother gave birth to a beautiful, blond baby at 544 Derrick Road in Derrick City, Pennsylvania during the 1920s. The child was so precious, the mom kept her with her at all times, day and night. Religiously, she tended to her needs and constantly doted over the sweet little girl.

The baby became livelier with each passing hour due to the attention she received. The woman, on the other hand, felt her energy wane. After three months without a break from her motherly duties, she lay down with the child one morning and lapsed into an exhausted slumber. In the course of her nap, she rolled over on the baby and smothered the life out of her despite her struggles and muffled bawling.

When the mother woke to find what she had done, she burst into tears and tore wildly at her knotted hair. Gathering up the child's corpse, she placed it gently on the floor and then ripped the sheets from her bed. In a daze, she tromped zombie-like up the steps to the attic where she hung herself from the rafters with those same cold sheets.

Since then, both residents and a summoned police officer have heard a baby's cries burst from a second story bedroom. No one has dared sleep in that room, either, due to the wailings and a rocking chair that rocks by itself. The protests of the child seem to reach a fever pitch around ten a.m.—the approximate time of her death.

MT. JEWETT'S POLTERGEIST DOCTOR

A physician lived at 23 East Main Street in Mt. Jewett, Pennsylvania. His office was where the sunporch is now. The rest of the house served as his residence until he died in his bedroom one thunder-racked night.

An old couple owns this beautiful home today. Their granddaughter moved in with them when she was six years old. She's the one who's haunted by that same doctor's ghost now that she occupies his old chamber. She's currently twenty-two, and according to her testimony, the specter has become dangerous!

The ghost especially hates objects with religious significance. The young woman had a praying hands statue once owned by her great grandmother sitting on her dresser. It lifted suddenly from its resting place and flew past her head to slam into the wall. Yes, and Christmas also upsets the deceased physician. He regularly knocks ornaments off the family tree and smashes them to bits on the carpet.

The phantom loves to creak open doors in the house, too, and then slams them violently shut, usually three times in succession. One evening, the girl went down to the basement to fetch canned goods for her grandmother. A screwdriver levitated from a shelf to zip by her and bury itself in the wall. As if that wasn't scary enough, she's seen the doctor's apparition numerous times in her room.

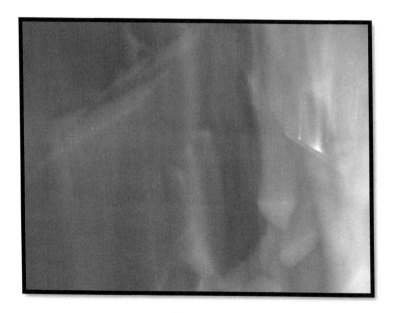

Being a devout man, the grandfather denies that these happenings are paranormal. He says the wind blowing through open windows causes them—even in winter when the windows are shut. Grandma, though, believes in the hauntings after being the victim of ghostly pranks. Often, she'll set down her coffee cup, for example, only to find it moved to another room.

The ladies recently hung crosses on the ground floor walls to keep the poltergeist upstairs. Now, when the girl's friends come to visit her, they refuse to go up to her bedroom. Some have become so frightened that they ran right out of the house!

HENRIETTA ROAD

To find Henrietta Road, travel north on Route 219 from Ashford Hollow toward Springville, New York. Instead of taking a sharp right to continue onto the four-lane stretch of 219, go straight for about a half-mile. Henrietta Road is on the left with an old cement plant at the foot of it.

Henrietta begins as a paved lane as it twists around a sharp bend and then straight up a hill past a farm and a cemetery. Shortly after, it becomes a narrow dirt track flanked by cornfields before coming to a dead end near some dense woods. It's best not to drive here after dark due to the deep potholes, darting deer, and two male entities that haunt the road.

The first is that of a young boy who drown in a nearby pond. He's eerie beyond belief, because of his water-bleached skin and the lily pads and sphagnum moss tangled around his legs. He's hurrying home to the cemetery down the road and looks neither left nor right as he scurries along, dripping wet. His eyes are open, but he won't see you drive past. It won't matter how many times you hit the high beams!

The other ghost wrecked his motorcycle while bouncing through a deep rut. The machine skidded on its side, grinding its rider to hamburger. He is now seen limping dazedly along the dirt track. He won't try to hitch a ride or appear in anyone's car. His injuries hurt too much as every inch of flesh was flayed from his left side during the gruesome accident.

RANDY'S UP THE RIVER

Randy's Up the River is located on Nine Mile Road in Allegany, New York. According to the owner, Randy Korkowicz, the name comes from the dire straits he and his wife, Debbie, would have found themselves in had their establishment not succeeded. They literally would have been "up the river without a paddle."

Randy's is a tavern, restaurant, and sports bar all wrapped into one with a TV blaring in every corner. The décor features plain wood paneling with red and brown striped curtains hanging over the windows. In the main dining area neon O'Doul's, Busch, and Harp Lager beer signs glare from the dark walls. Strings of Christmas lights add to the garishness of the room.

Besides being a haunt for students from nearby St. Bonaventure University, the bar is home to several actual ghosts. Korkowicz has been plagued by them for years. Often, he will deadbolt the doors for the night only to return later to find them unlocked. Another time, after last call, he was doing paperwork in his basement office when he heard footsteps upstairs. The doors were all locked on that occasion, but he found no one else in the building. Also, when a certain type of liquor was placed on the top shelf in the bar, the bottles got pushed off to smash on the floor. According to Randy, the "accidents" only stopped after another alcohol was displayed there.

The scariest event Randy experienced occurred at nine o'clock one morning. He reported to work early to change the oil in the fryers and was the first person there. He had just entered the kitchen and bent over to begin the task when someone hissed his name. The male voice was so close to his right ear that the breath of it moved his hair. He leaped up, spun around, and then fled into the parking lot after finding no one behind him. "That got me right there. That was something!" he later confessed to an *Olean Times Herald* reporter.

Mrs. K. has had weird encounters, too. Many times she and her staff have seen a gaunt man enter a downstairs door near the stairway leading to the second story. They never hear him climb the steps, though, or see him come around the corner to the bar. Dressed in a pair of jeans and a plaid shirt, he simply vanishes.

Randy's place was built around 1869 and originally served as a hotel and stagecoach stop.

During the Prohibition Era of the 1920s, it morphed into a speakeasy and brothel operated by Ma Reesnor. During an investigation of the premises, a member of the Southern Tier Paranormal Research Team believes that she saw one of Ma's girls peering out an upstairs window. Upon returning a second time, the ghost hunter and her associate ventured upstairs to explore the rooms that are now used for storage. Again, she spotted the girl at the same window but couldn't capture her on film. Her friend didn't see the apparition. She did, however, catch a whiff of stale perfume.

Going into another bedroom farther down the hall, the women had a terrifying experience. They were taking pictures of two white Christmas trees blocking the middle of the floor when a male voice growled, "Get out!" One investigator didn't hear the command and got pushed from the room by something "that blew right through her." The women immediately fled downstairs and haven't been back since!

DUDLEY HOTEL

With the railroad boom of 1868, Salamanca, New York was growing by leaps and bounds. To take advantage of the constant influx of passengers and railroad workers, Charles H. Dudley built a three-story hotel at the corner of Church and Main Streets that he dubbed the Dudley House.

Unfortunately, the structure was made of wood and susceptible to fire. In 1880, a great conflagration began in the washroom and quickly spread to twenty-eight nearby restaurants, banks, hardware stores, and lawyer's offices that quickly burned to the ground. Most thought the fire was caused by an overturned oil lamp. Some whispered that two ne'er-do-wells, who had been arrested the night before, threw lit rags in a window as an act of revenge.

Charles Mauer of Buffalo rebuilt the Dudley House out of bricks for $125,000 at 132 Main Street, its present location. This version of the hotel boasted fifty-two sleeping rooms, a parlor, a dining room, and a bar. The interior was furnished with only the best Brussels carpets and walnut chamber sets that attracted customers in droves.

Dudley Hotel, Salamanca, N. Y.

After Charles Dudley died in 1889, the establishment was sold to the Torge family in 1901. Disaster struck again in 1913 when a second fire gutted the Dudley. Of unknown origin, it started in the basement and took the efforts of four fire companies to extinguish. After the building was refurbished, it was renamed the Hotel Dudley.

George Kissack bought the business in 1960. He was known as a true "character" and lavishly remodeled the interior of the building, adding a banquet hall in the rear. He called the lounge the "Rondel Room," because it featured a chandelier constructed of Rondel glass he imported from Italy. As rumor had it, debauchery also occurred in his Dudley Motor Hotel. Hookers were reputedly imported from Buffalo, and gambling was rampant.

Kissack came to a bad end in 1977 due to an extramarital affair he had with a woman in Florida. His girlfriend took him to court to claim "damages." When he won the civil suit she had filed against him, she whipped out a pistol and shot him dead in front of the judge and gasping gallery. "You'll never cheat another person!" she wailed after firing the lethal bullets.

Kissack's ghost now wanders the halls of the Dudley that closed in 2014 and sits vacant. A dead maintenance man has also been seen performing his duties in the basement. When the hotel was still in operation, customers often reported a knock at their door by a phantom caller. The hall was always empty after the knock was answered. Others would go for a bucket of ice only to find the television turned off and their windows closed when they returned. The specter of Dave Varner was seen often, too. A railroad worker from Punxsutawney, Pennsylvania, he was identified by his distinct round body and striped bib overalls.

When Gloria Johnson was manager of the Dudley in the 1980s, she asked local psychic, Anita Cimbricz, to conduct an investigation. The medium went through the entire building room-by-room. Afterward, she swore that at least a dozen ghosts haunt the premises.

According to Jim Griffith, city historian, the lobby was the scene of the scariest event that occurred at the Dudley. The desk clerk and two waitresses were chatting there when they heard the elevator descend to the ground floor. The doors opened and out stepped a dapper gent dressed in an old-fashioned suit. The gent took five steps toward the front door only to disappear before their eyes. The spooked employees immediately sought out the manager, who had installed a closed circuit television surveillance system. When they checked the camera, they saw the elevator doors slide open. With cries of disbelief, they found no one inside!

AMERICAN LEGION POST 535

American Legion Post 535 is located at 67 Wildwood Avenue in Salamanca, New York. It is known as the Hughes-Skiba Post, because it's named for the first Salamanca soldiers killed in action in World War I and World War II. It's also haunted by numerous spirits!

The building was originally owned by Charles Gibson, a prominent citizen of the city. He made his fortune through railroad construction and then started the first mail order liquor company in the United States. He also organized the Salamanca Volunteer Fire Department and served as its chief. He died at home at the age of eighty-one from a prolonged illness he suffered after falling and fracturing his left thigh. During paranormal investigations, his specter is the most powerful. His voice resonates loudly from any Phasma Box.

Charles and his wife had a daughter and a son. The daughter, Vesta, was quite homely. She had stringy hair, a sloped brow, and a big nose. To prevent her from becoming an old maid, Charles arranged for her to marry Elsworth Terrill who had come to town from New Jersey to work as a railroad clerk. Terrill was a World War I hero whose arm had been blown off in combat. After his injury, he continued to lob grenades at the Germans with his left hand and was awarded the Distinguished Service Citation in 1919 for his bravery. He had to be even braver to marry Vesta. She was eleven years older than he despite the phony birthdate she scrawled on their marriage certificate.

A daughter was born to Elsworth and Vesta in 1922. She was also named Vesta. After Elsworth split two years later, the females lived alone in the family mansion. The mother homeschooled her girl, and they very seldom went out. The death of her father, Charles, made the older Vesta quite depressed. To make matters worse, she lost most of her income when the family liquor business was closed during Prohibition. The final straw came when her daughter turned seventeen and was due to leave Salamanca for finishing school.

The night before she was to board the train, the girl went to bed early suffering from cramps. She had just applied a heating pad when her mom stumbled into her room brandishing a .32-caliber revolver. Before she could even protest, a bullet bored through her forehead and blew out her brains. Her mother, meanwhile, turned and fled down the hall to the bathroom. With a sad smile, Vesta turned the gun on herself and shot a fatal hole in her right temple. The date of the murder-suicide was September 2, 1939.

It wasn't until nine days later that the bodies were discovered. Vesta's brother, Willard, noticed the newspapers piled up on their doorstep and went inside to investigate. The stench wafting from upstairs was so overpowering that Willard immediately called the police. The daughter's corpse was especially in bad shape, because her heating pad had been going all that time.

To this day, visitors to 67 Wildwood Avenue swear they catch a whiff of death. Lights come on and turn off by themselves, too, as the Vestas' ghosts flit from room to room. As can be expected, cold spots accompany them wherever they go.

There was also an attic light that snapped on by itself. The caretakers of the house would turn the light off only to see it shining from the window after they emerged onto the street. An electrician was hired to check the attic wiring but found nothing wrong. After police were summoned to inspect the upstairs, the third floor window was boarded up for good reason.

To rid themselves of morose memories, the Gibson family donated Charles' old house to the American Legion. According to Tammy Cummings, the club steward and paranormal expert, a new addition was built in the 1970s, and the barroom now sits where the backyard was located. She doubts that any of the Gibson ghosts ever venture down there, for in life they rarely left their residence.

Instead, there's a whole new set of specters that haunt the club. Cummings believes that most of them are past commanders who stop by for a visit. Often, shadows or the vapor of a person have been seen by customers.

Tammy has had several encounters after closing time, as well. The one she remembers most happened while she was cleaning the men's room. She had just bent over to wipe down the sink when her ponytail got yanked hard. She wasn't frightened, though, because she's curious about the supernatural and finds it exciting. She visits the Vestas' graves in Wildwood Cemetery on the anniversary of their deaths each year, too, and always leaves flowers.

SALAMANCA RAIL MUSEUM

The museum situated at 170 North Main Street in Salamanca, New York contains a wealth of information about the golden age of rail travel when railroads were the major means of transportation between cities. Displays of memorabilia focus on the three railways that served the area: the Erie, the Baltimore & Ohio, and the Buffalo, Rochester & Pittsburgh lines.

The museum itself is a completely restored passenger depot that was built in 1912 by the BR&P Railway. It features a ticket office that includes the original furniture and telegraph keys. There's also an authentic waiting room, baggage room, and ladies retiring room. Visitors have the opportunity to explore several onsite railroad cars, as well. These include a World War

II troop sleeper, a flatbed car, a crew car, and three cabooses.

A paranormal team sensed strong presences in these cars and also in the freight house occupied by a belligerent male entity. Several times in the foulest language he's cursed entering workers and told them they weren't wanted there. He also pushed museum director, Jare Cardinal, from behind. She stumbled, fell, and smashed her left hand in a piece of machinery.

The malicious spirit, Mary, lurks in the depot, too. She manifested herself during a cleanup session performed by a group of volunteers. One of the volunteers was a pragmatic businessman named Mike. While moving a wooden bookcase in the gift shop, he had it suddenly toppled down on him. As the shelf fell, several witnesses watched in amazement as a toy railroad car flew across the room to land on another shelf. Then they scrambled to free Mike from his predicament while he flailed his limbs and cried for help.

A few weeks later, another paranormal team scoured the depot with Mike and others in tow. When they entered the gift shop, they began an EVP session by asking, "Are you the one who knocked the bookcase down on Tom?"

"No!" snarled a woman's voice when the EVP was played back. "It was Mike!"

Upon hearing the chilling response, Mike cleared his throat nervously. Afterward, he wheezed, "I never believed in this paranormal stuff. Until *now*! Excuse me, folks. I'm outta here!"

DEWITTVILLE POOR HOUSE CEMETERY

The Chautauqua County Poor House was established in 1831 when the board of supervisors bought ninety acres of land in Dewittville, New York for $900. The following year, a brick house ninety-four feet long by thirty-two feet wide was built by George Hall to shelter 100 paupers.

The poor farm became a haven for the county's sick, blind, abandoned, abused, and insane. They were clothed, fed, and given meaningful work to earn their keep. Their children were provided a proper education, as well, and a doctor visited them daily to care for their needs. A second structure was raised in 1850, specifically for the insane.

Over 4,000 paupers were assisted before the county home relocated to a new facility at Dunkirk in 1961. The Dewittville buildings were sold to a private individual who promptly demolished them. That left the cemetery as a sole reminder of the property's history.

The potter's field had been opened in 1833 where deceased residents were buried in unmarked graves. It wasn't until 1864 that graves were marked with rectangular numbered stones. Round numbered stones were used later until the cemetery was filled to capacity in 1918, also with members of the community.

Soon after the poor farm was knocked down, its graveyard became a hotbed of paranormal activity. Glowing balls of light began flitting about the grounds, aimlessly searching for their destroyed home. Cries came from the darkness, too, to bemoan the loss of the only place the paupers weren't considered outcasts.

KING HOUSE

A middle-aged couple from New Jersey drove to Westfield, Pennsylvania on a house hunting trip. The husband and wife, both law enforcement officers, were tired of their dangerous jobs and hectic city life. They wanted to move to the country for some peace and quiet. What they found was even more frightening than anything they'd faced in police work!

A real estate agent took them south down Route 249 to show them a large brick house that sat perched atop King Hill near the local golf course. After unlocking the front door, the realtor stepped back and rasped, "Look around all you like, folks. I'll be waiting for you in the car."

As the couple approached the King House, they swore they heard a little girl's laughter. That didn't seem likely, considering that the place had been deserted for years. The wife took a few photos of the outside of the old mansion, but her camera stopped working when they went inside. While replacing the batteries, she saw a door leading to the cellar and took it.

The wife had just descended into the basement when she heard a furtive movement at the top of the stairs behind her. She knew it wasn't her husband, because he didn't like creepy places after all the crime scenes he'd investigated as a police officer. Although she couldn't see anyone, she took a photo anyway. Glancing at the digital picture, she discovered a young girl staring down at her.

The woman was a self-professed witch and had experienced many brushes with the supernatural. Flashing a thin smile, she waved at the ghost and then turned to explore the basement. It was musty, dank, and filled with curiosities. She also got a strong feeling that it had been used as a terminal for the Underground Railroad back in the day. An ominous atmosphere pervaded the place, and she knew it was time to return upstairs when a blue orb suddenly appeared and began circling her head.

Later that evening, the husband was exploring Joyce Tice's Tioga County history website to learn more about the King House. What he found bothered him so much that he called in sick and didn't report for work the next day. One of the pictures he stumbled across was of a King family reunion from the 1800s. Standing next to her father was the same little girl who his wife had photographed in the basement. She had on the same long dress and wore the identical barrettes in her hair!

GROVE RUN

Grove Run is an isolated valley near Sinnemahoning, Pennsylvania in Cameron County where stone was quarried and straight trees harvested for ship masts in frontier times. It was also the perfect place to build a dynamite plant. In 1905, businessman, Henry Auchu, organized the Sinnemahoning Powder Company there. George Jones designed and constructed the facility. The plant produced the usual grades of dynamite, and a nitro-cotton factory was added in 1907 to make the business self-sufficient.

On June 26, 1907, however, disaster struck! An accident occurred in the mixing room, and the resulting explosion rocked the powder mill, wrecking it in an instant. Five men were also blown to bits. They included foreman, J.D. Nelson; Edward Cole; Fillmore Summerson; and two sixteen-year-olds—Harry Cole and Samuel Shadman. Their corpses were so mutilated, they were hard to identify.

Today, the spirits of these mangled workers reside at a family home built not far from the factory ruins. This four-story manor has plenty of space for them all. There's a walk-in basement, a main floor with a balcony, a third floor bedroom suite, and a master bedroom and bath on the fourth floor. The latter is reached by an elevator that the teen ghosts love to ride.

The house is located at the very end of Grove Street after it turns to dirt. The property is posted and gated to keep intruders out. That obviously didn't work with the deformed phantoms who regularly spook the family and their maintenance staff.

Cody Ball, for example, was given a key to clean house while the owners were away. She was down on her hands and knees scrubbing a floor when she heard a sudden thump in the bedroom above her. The sound was so loud and terrifying that Cody immediately fled the building. She didn't bother dumping out her mop bucket, either, and quit this side job—permanently!

KINZUA CREEK

Since Bob Whiteman retired, he spends most of his time trout fishing. One of his favorite streams is Kinzua Creek in McKean County Pennsylvania. He especially likes to start at Route 219 and fish upstream to Guffey. This is an "artificial lures only" area, and Bob has hauled in many browns, brookies, and rainbows using a trout magnet where once banned night crawlers and salted minnows were quite effective.

On one such fishing trip, Bob and his two brothers drove up to Guffey on a dirt road paralleling the creek. Just before reaching the bridge there, they came to a straight stretch with a clear hundred-yard view of the brook below. A man in a pair of red shorts and a white t-shirt was standing on the bank in plain sight staring into the water. One second he was there. The next, he was gone!

All three fisherman witnessed the gents' disappearance and boiled out of their vehicle to go look for him. They were afraid he slipped into the creek and hurt himself. Strangely enough, they found no boot tracks or any other visible sign that a human being had been there.

Suddenly, Bob remembered what he had found near the stream a few weeks earlier during a hard rain. He saw something glistening near the rising creek water and mistook it for someone's tackle box. He thought he'd better rescue it before it washed away. When he reached the object, though, he found himself staring at a handmade placard with a warning scrawled on it: "As you wander to and fro. Beware the ghost of Tally Ho!"

With a shiver, Bob signaled his brothers. Then he hustled back to their truck as fast as his feet would carry him.

RIVERVIEW CEMETERY

Riverview Cemetery sits on a hillside overlooking Willow Bay in Warren County Pennsylvania, a mere 100 yards from the New York State line. The best way to reach it is to take Route 346 from Bradford, PA and continue onto State Highway 280 in Cattaraugus County NY. The entrance is located on the left.

Over 300 Native Americans are buried in this remote graveyard. They were moved there when lands promised to them "forever" were flooded by the Kinzua Reservoir in 1965. When their original resting place was disturbed at the Cornplanter Tract Cemetery, nests of timber rattlers were unearthed with them. Hissing horribly, the snakes rained down on the startled gravediggers, who feverishly exited their backhoes.

Chief Cornplanter is the most famous Seneca supposedly relocated to the Riverview Cemetery. Despite his request that his grave remain unmarked, in 1866 Pennsylvania erected a monument over it. This monument was the first to honor a Native American in the United States and was carefully moved to its present site.

Many Iroquois believe that Cornplanter's bones are buried elsewhere. That doesn't prevent visitors from flocking to his stone pillar near Willow Bay to leave feathers, coins, and bead jewelry. They wish to show their respect for the fierce warrior who led his tribe through the turbulent era of the American Revolution.

Several incidents of a supernatural nature have occurred at Riverview, as well. One woman swears that a wraith shot straight through her when she reached to open the graveyard gate. A group of noisy teens got their nerves jangled, too, while visiting one dark, windless night. After hearing a shed door open and bang shut repeatedly, they discerned the wild clopping of hooves heading toward them. They broke and ran, with the hooves closing ever closer, until they leaped in their car and sped away. Was it a herd of stampeding deer that found the kids' presence offensive? Or bucks like those that stand upright observed at sacred places like Ga'Hai Hill?

ABOUT THE AUTHOR

Hi, I'm Bill Robertson. I don't consider myself a spooky guy. I just like visiting haunted places and learning their history. I discovered the supernatural at an early age when my Swedish grandmother told me folktales about trolls and witches. She said that trolls would ride you to the ground and suck away your soul! My dad was extremely well-read, and he urged me in junior high to peruse the work of Edgar Allan Poe. I was especially impressed by the eerie settings Poe wove into his stories. It was the Gothic rock of the Doors, though, that hooked me on the horror genre. Their organ-mad music and tortured vocals had an irresistible appeal, as did Jim Morrison's dark imagery. To learn about my writing, visit **http://www.thehorrorhaven.com**.

BOOKS BY WILLIAM P. ROBERTSON

Short Story Collections

Lurking in Pennsylvania (2004), *Dark Haunted Day* (2006), *Terror Time* (2009), *The Dead of Winter* (2010), *Season of Doom* (2013), *Terror Time 2nd Edition* (2013), *Stories from the Olden Days* (2015), *Misdeeds and Misadventures* (2016), *More Stories from the Olden Days* (2017), *Love That Burns* (2017), *War in the Colonies* (2018), *Fear Is Forever* (2018), *Fun in the Olden Days* (2018), *Come In* (2019), *Ghosts Revisited* (2020), *Ghosts Revisited 2* (2021), *Ghosts Revisited 3* (2022), *More War* (2022).

Novels

Hayfoot, Strawfoot: The Bucktail Recruits (2002), *The Bucktails' Shenandoah March* (2002), *The Bucktails: Perils on the Peninsula* (2006), *The Bucktails' Antietam Trials* (2006), *The Battling Bucktails at Fredericksburg* (2006), *The Bucktails at the Devil's Den* (2007), *The Bucktails' Last Call* (2007), *Ambush in the Alleghenies* (2008), *Attack in the Alleghenies* (2010), *This Enchanted Land: The Saga of Dane Wulfdin* (2010), *The Bucktail Brothers of the Fighting 149th* (2011), *The Bucktail Brothers: Brave Men's Blood* (2012), *The 190th Bucktails: Catchin' Bobby Lee* (2014), *Annihilated in the Alleghenies* (2016), *Ambush in* the Alleghenies 2nd Edition (2021), *Annihilated in the Alleghenies 2nd Edition* (2022).

Videos

Ghosts (2020), *Gothic Poetry Slam* (2021), *Gothic Poetry Slam 2* (2021), *Gothic Poetry Slam 3* (2021).

Poetry Volumes

Burial Grounds (1977), *Gardez Au Froid* (1979), *Animal Comforts* (1981), *Life After Sex Life* (1983), *Waters Boil Bloody* (1990), *1066* (1992), *Hearse Verse* (1994), *The Illustrated Book of Ancient, Medieval & Fantasy Battle* Verse (1996), *Desolate Landscapes* (1997), *Bone Marrow Drive* (1997), *Ghosts of a Broken Heart* (2005), *Icicles* (2018), *Lost* (2018).

Audio Books

Gasp! (1999), *Until Death Do Impart* (2002), *Bucktail Tales* (2013).

Photo Books

Tombstones & Shadows (2019), *Graveyards: Glorious & Ghostly* (2019), *Abandoned Dwellings* (2019), *The Pennsylvania Bucktails* (2019), *An Eye for the Eerie* (2019), *Ghosts* (2019), *Ghosts II* (2020), *Ghosts III* (2020), *Serene Vistas* (2020), *Enter Winter* (2021).

E-Books

The above titles marked with a star (*) are also available in Kindle, iPad, and Nook e-book formats. *The Bucktail Brothers Series* combines both *The Bucktail Brothers of the Fighting 149th* and *The Bucktail Brothers: Brave Men's Blood* into one e-book.